BRIAN BROWN

Rodale books may be purchased for business or promotional use or for special sales. For information, please write to: Special Markets Department, Rodale Inc., 733 Third Avenue, New York, NY 10017
Printed in the United States of America
Rodale Inc. makes every effort to use acid-free ♾, recycled paper ♻.

Book design and illustrations by Nathan Love LLC
www.nathanlove.com

Library of Congress Cataloging-in-Publication Data on file with the publisher

ISBN 978-1-60961-568-0 (paperback)
Print number: 1
June 2012
RRD Crawfordsvlle, IN

Distributed to the trade by Macmillan

2 4 6 8 10 9 7 5 3 1 paperback

We inspire and enable people to improve their lives and the world around them.
rodalebooks.com

RINGFORCE™

"The most important thing in the Olympic Games is not to win but to take part, just as the most important thing in life is not the triumph but the struggle. The essential thing is not to have conquered but to have fought well."

—Baron Pierre de Coubertin,
founder of the modern Olympics

CONTENTS

THE KID FROM BROOKLYN

Booker was flying. Well, not really flying. But it felt that way when he ran at full speed. There was no other feeling like it: his face warming, his hair lifting as he moved against the wind, his arms chopping the air, his legs moving so quickly it almost seemed like he was floating.

It was a feeling he wished he could share with someone. But Booker didn't think anyone would understand. Certainly not his friends.

They had been treating him in this really weird way ever since his father had died. He understood it a little bit. They didn't really know what to say to him, or how to make him feel better. And maybe he was a little bit to blame. He had been kind of a downer to be around. Not listening. Daydreaming.

But he didn't think they should be treating him like he had a horrible disease or something. And it really hurt when, all of a sudden, Nick and Brendan didn't save a spot for him in the basketball game at recess. A voice inside told him to say something like, "Thanks a lot guys, nice friends." But instead his body was trying to make him cry. At least he was able to stop it before anyone could see the tears beginning to wet his eyes.

Things were piling up on him. First, his dad. Now, his friends were kind of forgetting he was alive. But running could always make these feelings go away.

So he was flying as he tried to keep up with the bus he usually took home with the rest of the kids. *Why take the bus when it would only make me feel worse to be around Nick and Brendan?*

Booker knew they could see him as he darted left and right along Atlantic Avenue. The sidewalks were choked with the usual obstacles: moms pushing strollers, plodding old people, and the slightly hunched homeless guys who could make you feel really, really sad deep inside.

And these guys usually didn't say anything... other than mumbling to themselves.

"Nice form, young man."

Booker slowed to look back. That was odd:

Homeless guy who looked ancient, but sounded so alive.

Booker refocused, and zoomed ahead.

He knew everyone on the bus was probably looking at him, making fun of him, but he suddenly didn't care what the other kids thought anymore.

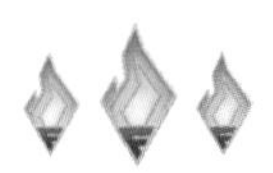

*WHEN YOU BELIEVE IN YOUR DREAM...
ALL IS POSSIBLE.*

That was the message on a poster of Muhammad Ali hanging on Booker's bedroom wall. It was a black-and-white photo of Ali standing triumphantly over a fallen and stunned Sonny Liston. It had been a birthday gift from his dad.

"Booker, do you know who this is?" his dad asked.

"Kind of," he said.

"He's the greatest boxer of all time... and you know how he got started?"

"Let me guess," Booker said. "The Olympics."

"Yup. That's right. Another Olympian. Gold. 1960, Rome... but what came before that?"

"I know... I know... hard work," Booker replied.

"You got it."

Booker's dad had a thing for the Olympics, and for hard work. He told Booker all the time that the greatest athletes were also the hardest working.

"When Ali was your age, he'd race his school bus as part of his training."

"No, he didn't."

"Yes, Booker, he most certainly did."

Everyone called him Booker, but his real name was Henry Garcia. His dad told him that even when he was little, he was always in a hurry, booking from place to place.

What his dad really wanted, and Booker knew this deep in his heart, was for Booker to be running fast for a reason... toward a goal... with a purpose.

That's why he liked to tell Booker stories about Olympians all the time—especially stories about Latino Olympians. He wanted Booker to be proud of his heritage.

"Do you realize Latino athletes have made an impact in almost every Olympic sport you can possibly imagine?... Like Pablo Morales, a law student, came out of retirement, and won gold in the butterfly at the 1992 Barcelona Olympics."

"Are there even Latino Winter Olympic athletes?" Booker asked.

"Sure. Jennifer Rodriguez and Derek Parra, just to name a few. They were roller skaters who turned into speed skaters."

"Anybody as good as Jesse Owens?"

"Well, have you ever heard of the great Cuban runner, *El Caballo*?"

"The horse?"

His dad laughed. "Yes, The Horse. That's what people called Alberto Juantorena. At the 1976 Montreal Olympics, he became the first and only athlete ever to win gold in the 400 and 800 meters... But to answer your question, no Latino has won the 100 meters at the Olympics—but I know a kid who could get there someday!"

"You do?"

"I'm looking at him right now. Henry Booker Garcia—from Brooklyn, New York."

Hoping that he'd someday make his dad proud, Booker pushed himself a little harder, lifting his legs even higher. He just had to beat that bus to his apartment.

Booker was running faster than he had ever run before. So fast, he was even keeping pace with the elevated subway as it roared on the tracks above him!

Wow, he thought, *I can actually get home faster by NOT taking the bus!*

Booker raced up the four floors to his apartment, like he usually did, leaping two steps at a time. His dad would always race him up the stairs. And not too long before his father died, Booker started to beat him to the top.

Maybe one day he would know what it would feel like to be one of those Olympic sprinters he watched on television... to know what it was like to become the world's fastest man, like Jesse Owens or Usain Bolt.

He could hear the announcer now:

"THERE'S THE KID FROM BROOKLYN, FASTER THAN A CITY BUS, JUST LOOK AT HIM GO!"

And then came perhaps the best part of all: the awarding of the gold medal... as the crowd cheered from the stands, getting louder... and louder... and louder...

MILK RUN

"Meow... MEOW!"

Booker quickly snapped out of his daydream of Olympic glory.

Max was licking his hand with that coarse tongue of his, letting Booker know just how hungry he was.

Strange, thought Booker, *didn't Mom feed him?*

Max slinked over to the refrigerator, where a note from Mom was stuck to the door. It was written in big, black letters:

BUY MILK AND CAT FOOD.
LATE NIGHT AT WORK.
MAKE YOURSELF DINNER.
LOVE, MOM

Booker was suddenly slammed back to reality. Bad enough he had to go to the store right away because otherwise Max was going to be climbing all over him and clawing at his head and making a kind of long, demanding MEOOOOWW that was really, really annoying.

BUY MILK AND CAT FOOD.
LATE NIGHT AT WORK.
MAKE YOURSELF DINNER.
LOVE, MOM
P.S. JOIN THE TRACK TEAM. COACH KEEPS CALLING.
P.P.S. DO YOUR MATH HOMEWORK FIRST!

Bad enough he had to make his own dinner. Yes, yes, he knew Mom had to work a lot harder since Dad died, but he was finally actually starting to get tired of microwaved gooey mac and cheese.

All that was bad enough, but Mom also added two other really, really annoying reminders.

> P.S. JOIN THE TRACK TEAM.
> COACH KEEPS CALLING.
> P.P.S. DO YOUR MATH
> HOMEWORK FIRST!

Ugh.

UGH.

Mr. Tweedy, his math teacher, was not a bad guy. In fact, he could even make math seem kind of cool and important.

"Ladies and gentlemen, we cannot take a measure of our world if we don't realize we live in a world of measurement. Our days are measured in hours. Our lives are measured in years. Our athletic champions are measured in minutes and seconds, feet and inches, meters and centimeters. When you know math, everything adds up—pun intended!"

Mr. Tweedy knew Booker's dad loved the Olympics, and lately he had been testing Booker's knowledge of Olympic stats. It made math fun, and also made Booker feel good about himself at a time when he needed a boost.

"How far was Bob Beamon's long jump at the 1968 Olympics?"

"29 feet," Booker answered.

"And..." said Mr. Tweedy. "AND?" he repeated even louder.

"Oh," said Booker, "29 feet... AND two and a half inches."

"Yes. Precision matters."

The track coach was a totally different story.

Coach Popov was born in Russia and was built like the Greek and Roman statues Booker had seen on a class trip to the Metropolitan Museum of Art.

"Booker!" he would bellow in the school hallway so everyone could hear. "When am I going to see you on the track? The team needs you! Come on! Where's your school spirit?"

Like, didn't the guy know his dad had died? School spirit? The school didn't care about HIS spirit.

"Booker, you could be another Jesse Owens... 1936 Berlin Olympics... four gold medals... showed Hitler that black athletes were champions, too!"

Everything about Coach Popov was full throttle, in your face, unstoppable. Supposedly, his workouts were so hard, some kids had actually hurled all over the place.

When Booker told his dad he didn't want to join a team with a coach that made you puke, his dad told him not to believe everything you hear.

"Booker," he said, "that's just a story made up by kids at school looking for an excuse to explain why they're too lazy to join the team."

APRIL

"Meow... M-E-E-O-W-W!"

Everything was so different since his dad had died. Everything was a little harder. A lot of things didn't make sense.

Booker let a single tear roll down his cheek before he wiped his eyes. He wished he could go back in time and race his dad up the steps again.

The dad that would give him a hug when he needed it the most.

me Deli
OLD CUTS • HOT COFFEE • MILK
OPEN 7 DAYS
ATM
ICE
PENNY FOR A DREAM

SUDDEN STORM

Booker headed to the small grocery store across the street from his apartment to buy milk and cat food for Max.

He grabbed the items and stood in line.

The woman in front of him was taking forever, and now the cashier was yelling at her.

"Hurry up, Grandma, I've got other customers. That's how much it costs! If you don't like our prices, shop somewhere else."

Booker got nervous. Did he have enough money? He added up the prices of the milk and cat food, and pulled a couple of crumpled bills from his pocket.

His stomach began to toss. He didn't have enough money!

Now a very, very, VERY hungry Max was going to be a very, very, VERY annoying cat. Math homework was already hard enough. And it would be that much more challenging with Max meowing every single second.

Just then, Booker felt a chill. It was a deep cold that reminded him of those painfully windy days walking along the East River in the middle of winter.

Only it was April, and the flowers were blooming, trees budding, bees buzzing.

The cold crawled up his spine, and he shivered all over.

Suddenly Booker was surrounded by a thick, chilly mist.

Maybe the store's refrigerated display case was malfunctioning. It was as if someone had accidentally turned the thermostat to the super Arctic cold setting.

That made sense. Well, not really.

"It's ok," a woman's voice said in a smooth, almost velvety tone. "Just take them. He won't see you. He's too busy."

Booker whipped around and caught a glimpse of a woman gliding away in an inky cloud of vapor.

He rubbed his eyes to make sure that they were working properly.

The woman had a cat following her. But not the kind like Max. It looked like one of those snow leopards that lived in the Himalayas, the ones that Booker had seen in the *Big Book of Cats* he had at home. But what was a snow leopard doing in a little grocery store in Brooklyn?

Then, from nowhere and everywhere, he heard that voice again.

"Booker," it said, slowly and confidently. "Go ahead. Take them. No one will see you."

She was so convincing. Who was this mystery lady? Should he listen to her? Should he take the milk and cat food?

He couldn't think straight... like his thoughts were drowning in black sludge.

"Max needs the cat food, Mom needs the milk," Booker said to himself.

He eyed the door.

"Hey, you!" the cashier yelled. "I know what you're thinking; you're up to no good!"

Booker was paralyzed. He dropped the cat food, and the milk slipped from his hand.

Oh no.

PLOP!

BOOM!

The milk carton exploded and milk splattered all over the place.

"Hey, you!" the cashier growled, "I'm going to... I'm going to... squash your tiny skull!"

As Booker bolted from the store, he thought: *I don't have a tiny skull.*

WHOA.

Right around the corner, there was a guy who had a *giant* head—like the size of a bowling ball! And he was wearing a plaid cap that was way too small.

The lunkhead was leaning against a limo. Not just any old limo—this one was smoking, like literally. It was oozing vapor.

It probably belonged to that strange lady in the store. But Booker wasn't going to wait to find out. The cashier was right behind him.

He sped toward the East River, knowing he could lose anyone in the park along the waterfront. There would be people walking dogs of all shapes and sizes... little kids dashing about like loose basketballs... and daredevil skateboarders dodging all the joggers.

Booker knew how to navigate this wonderful mess of energy that you find everywhere in New York City.

LOTTO · SODA
EAT

Booker was close enough now to see the park entrance. He was almost in the clear. What he hadn't counted on, though, was the return of the freaky limo with the big-headed driver.

Man, this dude was going to block his perfect escape route.

The car swerved and stopped in front of him. The back window rolled down with an electric hum, and he got his first good look at the mysterious lady from the grocery store.

Well, actually, not a good look, because she was more like a ghost emerging from a fog. All Booker could really make out were her eyes: glowing, greenish.

"Don't be afraid," she said soothingly. "Get in. I won't bite."

Yeah, right. That's exactly what he WASN'T going to do.

"Booker, you don't want to get in trouble with your mom, do you?"

As every kid knew, the one way to get in really, really BIG TROUBLE with your parents was to get in a car with a stranger.

"Don't be afraid... I'll take you back to the store. Explain it was all my fault. Okay?"

This lady seemed really clueless. Was she from, like, another century? And she wasn't just a stranger. She was a really strange stranger.

Booker started to feel that freezing sensation again as he slowly backed away.

"I... I'll just walk home on my own."

It was now so cold he could see his breath.

"Okay," said the ghostly mystery lady in a tone that wasn't so sweet anymore. "We'll just do this the hard way."

In a flash, the driver was out of the car. He ran straight for Booker, with a surprising burst of speed for a big lunkhead who weighed, like, 400 pounds or something.

Booker took off.

He headed for the Brooklyn Bridge, where the caveman with the stupid-looking cap would be slowed by a crush of pedestrians and a mess of rush-hour traffic.

"Give up, kid!"

The caveman was right behind him. Booker could hear him huffing.

And then, as if this day wasn't weird enough, it started to snow. In the middle of April!

Kind of cool, Booker thought. But the snow

thickened, the wind howled, the temperature plummeted.

"Got you now, kid!"

Booker felt a hand grabbing the back of his shirt, but the caveman couldn't hold on. Booker was just moving too fast, and the sidewalks were getting slicker.

Booker heard the THUD of a large-bodied human meeting the ground, but he kept going. The howling wind sent snowflakes smack into his eyes, and he couldn't see anything.

"Booker!... BOOKER! Grab my hand!"

A girl with sky-blue eyes and rosy cheeks emerged from the white on white. She was just inches from his face. He had never been this close to a girl who was so pretty... so glowing with life.

"WHERE DID YOU GO?" the caveman yelled, searching for Booker in the blinding snow.

"Put these on," the girl commanded, handing him a pair of cross-country skis.

"I've never skied."

"Well, you better learn fast... Watch me. Slide right. Slide left."

"Where are we going?"

"Across the bridge."

"Why are we doing that?"

"Just hurry up, Booker!"

The caveman was still lost in the blinding snow, but seemed to be getting closer.

"KID! GIVE IT UP!"

"How do you know my name?" Booker asked the ski girl.

"Too many questions. And you need to go faster. I know you can."

New York has a lot of bridges, but none compare to the Brooklyn Bridge, which connects Brooklyn to Manhattan. It is poetry in stone and steel, with stately towers of double archways. When it was built more than a century ago, they even made a lane for people to walk across.

Now, many decades later, on that same pedestrian walkway, there were only two people making any kind of progress in the midst of a fierce, fast-forming surprise snowstorm that was bringing everything to an immediate halt.

"This has something to do with the spooky woman?" Booker asked the really cute but really serious stranger.

She nodded as she powerfully plowed ahead.

"My name's Ida," she said when they finally paused. "No more questions right now. You've got to keep going. Go to this address in Chinatown. Tell them your name."

She handed Booker a card.

SHANGHAI CHIANG
Corner of Pell and Doyers St.
Founded 1896

"Why aren't you coming with me?" Booker asked her.

"That lady in the limo—she has lots of ways to find all of us. We need to split up."

"All of us? Who's US?"

"No more questions. Trust me."

There was no good reason for Booker to trust this Scandanavian-looking ski girl who was sending him to a restaurant in Chinatown. No good reason at all.

Yet, he somehow believed she was making the most sense on the wackiest day of his life.

Maybe it was her determination, or her cool calm, or the sparkle in her sky-blue eyes.

"Are you from Sweden?"

"No, guess again."

"Norway?"

"Right!"

"Oh. Of course," Booker said, remembering how much his dad admired the great Norwegian Olympic athletes, like Vegard Ulvang.

"You're from the country with Vegard the Viking: the cross-country guy who raced with, like, frozen boogers dripping out of his nose."

"Yup," she said, smiling for the first time. Then, pushing off on her poles, she disappeared through the chunky flakes.

Shanghai Ch

CHINATOWN

As Booker approached Shanghai Chiang, the snow tapered off and the sun began to glow through the thinning clouds.

"Welcome, Mr. Garcia," said an extra-large waiter who appeared to be guarding the restaurant's front door.

This guy didn't look like any waiter Booker had ever seen before. He was humongous—tall, with a shaved head, wide shoulders, and muscular arms—and he had this deadly don't-mess-with-me look in his eyes.

He reminded Booker of the Shaolin monks Brendan never stopped talking about. These were monks who lived in the mountains of central China and supposedly invented Kung Fu.

Brendan said they could break strips of metal and blocks of wood with their heads. Booker thought this was another one of Brendan's famous fabrications. But Brendan insisted it was absolutely, positively the truth.

"I bet you know Ida," he said to the waiter.

"Of course."

"And you know about the lady who kind of looks like Angelina Jolie and has a snow leopard."

"Of course."

"And for some reason you know me even though I've never met you."

"Yes, Booker. I am sure you are a little mystified by what just happened. Go to the back of the restaurant. Open the door to the alley."

"What?"

"Go. The lady and her limo could get here at any minute."

Inside the restaurant, as Booker zigzagged around tables, he passed a giant photo of the very moment the torch was lit at the 2008 Beijing Olympics, a vast scene showing the rippling Olympic flag with the five interlocking rings: blue, yellow, black, green, and red... a parade of all the world's nations together in peace, blazing in a riot of colors.

And in the upper left of the photo, appearing to float on air, was the final torchbearer as he lit the rooftop cauldron at the Bird's Nest.

Booker tried to remember the name of that torchbearer. He knew he was a great Chinese Olympic gymnast. Which made sense. Gymnasts have to be pretty fearless people to be able to do what they do.

As Booker exited the restaurant into a lonely alley, he saw a hooded homeless man hunched over a fire burning in a large garbage can. The fire had a strange blue color.

"Wonderful, wonderful... you've made it," the man said.

Ordinarily, Booker would have done his best to avoid this kind of guy.

Except this was no ordinary day.

He'd never seen a fire burning blue. And at this point, he was desperate to understand what the heck was going on.

The man turned around. The hood covered his forehead, so it was hard to see his eyes. What Booker could see of the man's face had wrinkles on top of wrinkles.

"Booker, my name is Opa, and I am very pleased to meet you."

Though he looked like he was a million years old, his voice was rich and powerful—just like Coach Popov's.

"Have I seen you before?" Booker asked. He recalled the strange homeless man who had praised him as he was running home from school.

"Well, let's put it this way... I've known you since you were born... And I am sorry about your father. You should know he was right... The spirit is in you. You are capable of great things. But nothing great is accomplished without hard work. Without sacrifice. Without courage."

Booker began to feel a little dizzy again, like when all that stuff was happening at the grocery store: the old lady who couldn't pay for her groceries, the mystery woman trailed by an animal that belonged in a zoo, milk spraying everywhere.

"I know... I know... your cat is hungry... you left a large puddle of milk at the grocery store... you've got math homework... and you're going to be in big trouble with Mom."

Opa had read his thoughts. All of them.

"I'll be in even bigger trouble if I don't get home by the time Mom is back from work."

"Booker, please listen to me. Everything will be all right. I can make sure you get back home before your mom walks in the door."

"How?"

"I can't explain that now. There's no time."

"But that woman? She seemed like someone from another planet."

"Very perceptive, Booker. In fact, she is only a temporary visitor to this world. But you should know: she fears you more than you fear her."

"Am I dreaming? Is this real?"

"Even dreams can be real if you want them to be," Opa said. "So do you want to make your dreams come alive? It's your choice... life as it is, or life as you want it to be?"

Booker hesitated. He realized, somehow, that he was making a big decision.

"You must walk into the flame," Opa told him.

As Opa said these words, the blue flame rose higher from the garbage can. As it came closer to Booker, he instinctively stepped back... but this was a fire made only of light, not heat.

He took a deep breath, closed his eyes, and stepped forward.

Booker was flying again.

MOUNT OLYMPUS

"Welcome, Booker, to Mount Olympus!"

Booker was high above the clouds. Yet, higher still, a massive mountain scraped the sky above him. A stairway, lined by blazing torches and flanked by huge marble columns supporting godlike statues, rose to the summit.

What?
Is this real?

Even Opa looked different. He had been completely transformed, from a hunched, wrinkly figure to a man unlike any Booker had ever seen.

Opa was actually glowing, and he seemed taller than before. His long, golden hair was styled like those pictures of gods and Titans in Booker's *Guide to Greek Mythology*.

"I know, it's a lot to take in," he said to Booker with a gentle smile. "Let me show you around."

As they started to climb the stairs, Opa explained, "These statues honor legendary Olympians, stretching back thousands of years."

"Is there a statue of Muhammad Ali?"

"He's here, but a few centuries up the mountain. There's also a certain sprinter your school track coach likes to mention."

"Jesse Owens?" Booker asked.

"Indeed... a brilliant combination of speed and technique."

As they climbed, Booker saw dozens and dozens of children on the mountain. There were feverish soccer and rugby matches on lush green fields, sailboats and sculls skimming across a lake as clear as glass, and runners circling a track of soft orange clay.

Higher up there were courts for basketball and volleyball. Booker could hear the TOCK TOCK of table tennis, the THWACK of shuttlecocks, and the SPLASH of swimmers racing at full speed.

Near the top, it was frosty white. Booker squinted to see snowboarders soaring above a halfpipe and rocketing down the slope.

"There are more than 200 young athletes here, who are just like you," Opa told Booker. "They represent every nation on Earth, and they all have the same goals: *Citius. Altius. Fortius*."

"The Olympic motto," Booker immediately replied. His father used to repeat it to him at least once a week, but in English.

"Faster. Higher. Stronger. That's what all the great ones were thinking," his dad would tell Booker, "trying to improve themselves every day."

"Hey, Mr. Brooklyn!" a familiar voice shouted. "It's your friend from the land of the Vikings!"

Ida ran over and surprised Booker with a near-suffocating hug.

"So, I guess you found the Chinese restaurant?"

Ida was carrying a pair of speed skates, not skis this time, and was dressed in a kind of form-fitting superhero bodysuit meant to turn a human being into a speeding bullet.

"You were a natural on skis, Booker. I'd love to see you try the ice."

The shrill sound of a whistle pierced the air and interrupted their chat.

"Ida!... *Adrakse ti mera!* Seize the day!"

"Gotta go. That's my trainer. Like a Greek god, huh? Except he speaks Greek half the time, and I don't know what the heck he's saying."

As impressively chiseled as Coach Popov was, Ida's trainer could eat him for lunch and spit him out. Breathtakingly beautiful otherworldly people were everywhere in this otherworldly place called Mount Olympus... gods and goddesses... like in a movie.

"Booker," Opa explained, "our devoted teachers are known as guardians. Devoted to helping all of you search for the balance of a sound mind and a sound body."

As they continued up the mountain, Booker could see kids jumping and sprinting, lifting and leaping, soaring and twisting...

AND landing...

AND smiling... one of the sunniest smiles Booker had ever seen.

"Hello," said the young gymnast Booker had been watching.

She was trying to keep from giggling.

"I know what you are thinking. This is a dream, right? But I am saying to myself, 'This is the best dream of my whole life, and it is okay if I never wake up.' Right?"

"And," said Opa kindly, "would you like to tell Booker your name and where you are from?"

"Oh, ha ha," the girl chuckled, "I did not tell you, did I? My name is Desta. And I come from the beautiful highlands of Kenya, the birthplace of the ancestors of all humanity. And I want to be like Nadia Comaneci, the best Olympic gymnast ever."

"But Nadia also knew," Opa said, "that to be the best in competition requires great focus in practice."

"Booker," Desta whispered, "they are telling me I have trouble with concentration. And you know what? They are right!"

Booker smiled.

"But Opa," Desta said, "I am going to be very serious from now on."

"That's the spirit, Desta."

"*Asante*."

"You're welcome, Desta."

"*Asante*?" Booker asked.

"Thank you, in Swahili," Desta told him as she ran back to the gymnastics mat.

"And *tutaonana*!"

"What?"

"See you later!"

Opa led Booker over to the huffing and puffing and grunting of kids built like boulders. They were lifting barbells stacked with weights.

"Shen, here from China, is training to be the most powerful weightlifter of all time," said Opa.

The kid was twice as wide as Booker. He put down his weights and spoke slowly, his eyes frequently glancing downward.

"It is a pleasure to meet you," said Shen.

"Same here," Booker replied.

"And now I must go. I must return to my training."

Shen reminded Booker of his friends Nick and Brendan, who weren't really trying to be mean; they just didn't know what to say to him since his dad had died.

In Shen's case, he just seemed quiet by nature.

"Shen! Can you come back for a second?" Booker asked.

"Yes?"

"What's the name of the guy who was the final torchbearer at the Beijing Olympics? The guy who was flying in the air and lit the flame on top of the roof of the stadium?"

Shen's face brightened immediately.

"Booker, what a special moment for China! I was so proud. That was Li Ning. And he is a very important person in Chinese sports history. He won six medals in gymnastics at the 1984 Los Angeles Olympics."

"Wow."

"He is a hero to all of China," said Shen. "But, if I'm going to be a hero, too, I must get back to lifting weights."

“Of course,” said Booker. “Thanks... I understand.”

“Do you?” Opa asked.

“Do I... ?”

“Do you understand that heroes are made, not born?” Opa said.

“Maybe... kind of.”

“You have a gift, Booker. You are fast. And, like you, many of the legendary Olympians we honor here had wondrous natural abilities...

“But that’s not why we honor them. We honor them for the way they made the most of their gifts... By hard work. By listening. By learning from their mistakes.”

“I’m already faster than everyone in my school,” Booker said. “And I’ve always loved to run. And the more I run, the faster I get.”

“But,” said Opa, “you could be even *faster*.”

Booker’s guardian may not have looked like Coach Popov, but he certainly acted like him.

He barked instructions, told Booker he wasn’t trying hard enough, barely let him catch his breath.

“Let’s go, let’s go, Booker... let’s go again.”

His name was Sostratas, and he had Booker running the same short distance over and over.

“Speed alone does not win races, Booker. It is speed plus specific training. You don’t train for a marathon the same way you train for a sprint.”

"It seems like you're training me for a very, very short race," Booker said, his voice kind of raspy because he was breathing so hard.

"Yes, the *stade*," Sostratas explained. "It was the first event at the first ancient Games, almost 3,000 years ago. The race is the length of the first stadium in Olympia, Greece—about 200 meters."

Booker figured that was about the same distance as two city blocks.

"Sounds kind of easy."

"Be careful, Booker. That is a judgment best made AFTER you've raced."

The competition took place in a replica of that first stadium in Olympia: cozy, U-shaped, with only one feature—a track extending in a straight line without a curve.

Booker lined up with seven other runners.

"Run *through* the finish line," Sostratas said.

Booker wasn't sure what that meant. *Of course* he was going to run through the finish line.

"Do you understand?" Sostratas asked.

"Got it," said Booker, barely paying attention. He was pretty sure no other kid on Mount Olympus could possibly beat him.

And, indeed, Booker bolted out in front. Flying again—his face warming, his hair lifting as he moved against the wind, arms chopping the air, his legs moving so quickly it seemed like he was floating.

He looked quickly to his left and to his right, and saw that he had a comfortable lead... He imagined a TV announcer calling the race:

"THERE'S THE KID FROM BROOKLYN, LOOK AT THAT SMOOTH SPEED, HE'S GOING TO WIN THIS RACE... WITH EASE!"

With the finish line in sight, Booker raised his arms in celebration, slowing ever so slightly... then WHOOSH! Someone whizzed past him.

Booker had LOST.

In an instant, his exhilaration was replaced by bewilderment.

How did THAT happen?

He was bent over, his chest heaving. It was as if the shock of losing had made him extra exhausted... and kind of sick.

Booker felt a gentle tap on his back.

"Nice race, Garcia."

Booker looked up. It was the runner in green and gold shorts who had nipped him at the finish line. The kid from Jamaica.

"I didn't think I could catch you after that terrific start you had."

Booker shook his hand.

"I didn't think anybody could catch me, either."

"Sometimes, Garcia, it's easier to chase than to lead," the winner said, trying to make him feel a little bit better.

Sostratas was waiting for Booker as he walked off the track.

"You didn't listen to what I said, did you?"

"Yes, I did. You told me to run through the finish line."

"But you didn't run through the finish line, you slowed down. You thought you'd won the race before it was over."

Booker nodded and looked away, fighting back tears. How could he feel so many highs and lows in the same day?

"Come here," Sostratas said, wrapping him in a big hug.

It was the very best possible thing he could do for a kid experiencing his first great athletic disappointment... made worse because Booker had let himself be beaten in a competition he should have won.

KEEPING THE FLAME ALIVE

The sound of five trumpets pierced the night sky... Opa's signal that the Parade of Nations was about to begin.

Booker followed the other athletes to the top of Mount Olympus. He was wearing the red, white, and blue outfit that Opa had given him to represent his country.

Along the way, torches lined the polished stone stairway leading to the summit. At the top, a bright, blue flame burned against a deep, starry sky. It was somehow both day and night.

Leaning against a column, a snowboarder with a splash of long, blond hair called out, "Hey, mate!"

It seemed like he had springs for feet as he bounced over to meet Booker.

"So, you're the speedster from the Big Apple... New York City?"

"And you're a snowboarder from... let me guess... the land Down Under?"

"Yup, Australia, or as we put it: Oz. Largest island and smallest continent on Earth."

"So, can an Aussie be a Shaun White fan?"

"Of course. Double Olympic champion... 2006 Torino Winter Olympics, 2010 Vancouver Games... You know, he's been called The Flying Tomato because of his red hair... I was thinking maybe they could call me... The Leaping Lemon."

"Seriously?"

"Just kidding. My name's Wiri."

Wiri and Booker followed the other athletes to a majestic marble amphitheater that encircled the flame burning in a massive cauldron. Booker could see Shen in China's red and yellow... Desta in Kenya's red, green, and black... Ida in Norway's red and blue. This festival of colors reminded Booker of the dazzling plume of a peacock.

Opa called everyone to attention and took his place at the foot of the giant cauldron.

For the first time, Opa looked small.

"Welcome, all of you," Opa began. "The 204 of you represent every nation that is part of the

Olympic movement. Each of you has been chosen because of your burning desire to stretch the limits of what is possible. Each of you has the potential to be not just a great athlete, but a great leader.

"Look above me, in the night sky. Here are some of the great leaders from Olympic history."

Images appeared above them, making Mount Olympus a kind of outdoor movie theater.

"Decathlete Jim Thorpe... the star of the 1912 Summer Games in Stockholm... the greatest athlete of his age...

"Britain's man of principle... sprinter Eric Liddell...

"Babe Didrikson... who high-jumped, hurdled, and hurled the javelin... and demanded the world allow women to express themselves through sports...

"Marathoner Abebe Bikila... the first of many African wonders to come...

"Wilma Rudolph... who conquered childhood illness to become the world's fastest woman...

"Gymnast Olga Korbut... the teenager whose dazzle and charm changed her sport forever...

"And Dream Teams... in so many sports.

"In your world," Opa continued solemnly, "I am an invisible old man... But here, on Mount Olympus, I am known as Prometheus...

"Long ago, when darkness ruled the Earth, I stole light from the gods and gave it to humanity. Since then, the world has thrived in light, but dark forces are constantly trying to tip the balance. The eternal flame is forever fragile, and I cannot keep it lit on my own.

"The flame in this cauldron is a reflection of the light inside of each of you. That is why you are here. Each and every one of you was visited by Nyx... the goddess of darkness... the enemy of enlightenment. She can only exist in shadows, and strives to extinguish the light forever.

"Remember, she tried to pull each of you into darkness, but you found a way to overcome her tricks...

"It is only you... who... by choosing the path of sacrifice... and courage... and unity... can keep this flame on Mount Olympus alive... and the hundreds of flames courageously lit by the Olympic legends who came before you...

"It is, in the end, not the triumph, but the struggle...

"And Nyx will NEVER surrender..."

Booker felt a chilling breeze at his back, just as he had at the grocery store. The chill crawled up his spine, and he shivered all over.

Oh no. Not a good sign.

The ground started to shake, and the flame atop the giant cauldron began to flicker and shrink. An icy wind blew across the amphitheater.

Booker rushed to the edge of the summit. A thick, creeping fog seemed to be swallowing the ground below. He couldn't see the torches along the staircase anymore.

"Hey, Booker!" Ida yelled. She was at the cauldron lighting a torch.

"Catch!" she shouted, tossing it to Booker.

USA

The fog was gathering strength, snaking its way up the stairs toward Booker, suffocating the torches along the way.

Suddenly, the GROOOOWL of a wild cat filled the air.

Booker's hair stood on end.

Nyx's snow leopard leaped out of the fog.

"Go!" yelled Opa. "Keep the flames alive!"

Booker tightened his grip on the torch... and flew down the stairs.

He heard Desta shouting: "Booker! Cats, no matter how big, HATE fire. Give ME the torch."

As Desta ran up beside him, Booker was amazed that a small girl was prepared to scare off a cat ten times the size of Max.

"Give it to me," she ordered. "I'm from Kenya. This isn't the first time I've been face-to-face with a ferocious animal!"

Booker watched in admiration as she

fearlessly waved the torch like a fencer wields a sword, stepping forward, thrusting the fire at the big cat.

"Sorry, Mr. Leopard—we're not interested in being your dinner!"

The animal quickly retreated, hissing and whimpering, disappearing into the mist.

"NOOOO!..."

Nyx's deafening scream became a ferocious wind and a freezing rain, which instantly coated the stairs with super-slick black ice.

As Desta and Booker were struggling to stay on their feet, Shen appeared out of nowhere, planting himself like a tree trunk.

"Way to go, Shen!" Booker yelled over the roaring storm, as Shen's sheltering width allowed

them to push ahead. "You're our own Great Wall of China!"

Booker took the torch from Desta.

"Try to stay behind us!" he told her.

Now hailstones were bouncing off the steps, stinging their eyes.

And there was the BOOM and CRACK of thunder and lightning.

They had to make it down the stairway.

Suddenly, Shen surprised everyone as he forced himself to do something he had never done before. He shouted.

"DESTA!"

She had fallen and was slipping down the mountain. "HELPPPP!"

Wiri whizzed by them on his snowboard and rocketed toward Desta. But as Wiri was about to grab her, he heard the frightening RUMBLE of an approaching avalanche.

Wiri snatched Desta, and instead of trying to outrun the avalanche, he turned his snowboard into it, flying up, off and over the tumbling snow, as if it were the lip of a halfpipe.

"Nice air!" Booker remarked.

As Wiri's snowboard SHUSHED to a stop, Booker heard the SCRAPING sound of skates slashing the ice.

It was Ida.

"The flames are going out everywhere," she warned. "Nyx is getting more powerful by the minute."

"Your timing is absolutely perfect, as always," Booker said, handing her the torch.

Ida blazed down the icy stairway, relighting the flames that Nyx's storm had been rapidly snuffing out.

As each torch blazed anew, the darkness retreated, the wind settled, the hail quieted, the fog began to vanish...

And as the ice on the stairs began to melt... Ida's skates quickly became useless.

"Desta," Ida called out, her arms flailing. "I need your help!"

As if running toward a vaulting horse in gymnastics, Desta sped toward a tall column. And just before reaching it, she began a rapid tumbling sequence and her momentum launched her skyward.

Ida tossed the torch to Desta, and Desta... in that same fluid motion... caught it and reignited the flame.

With an exquisite sense of balance, Desta motored ahead, lighting more and more torches as she deftly descended the steep stairways.

The other four athletes raced down Mount Olympus right behind her. As they neared the main entrance gate at the foot of the mountain, Booker could see that Desta was tiring.

"You okay if I take it from here?" Booker asked.

Desta, breathing heavily, passed the torch with one of her shining smiles.

Booker was close to the bottom. Two blocks maybe. The length of the *stade*.

But what was that hulking mass coming straight at him? It was the hazy shape of a large man with a giant head who looked like Nyx's driver.

He wasn't stopping.

Booker wasn't stopping.

The caveman transformed himself into a bowling ball of ice.

WHOMP. SPLAT.

Booker was knocked flat.

Then he heard Nyx's oily, echoing voice.

"BOOKER...

"YOU'RE NOT SPECIAL... WHO ARE YOU KIDDING?

"YOU HAVE NO FRIENDS...

"YOUR FATHER ABANDONED YOU...

"AND YOU'RE A LOSER..."

Then he heard his dad's voice: *"When you believe in your dream, all is possible."*

And he remembered what Opa had said: *"Nyx fears you more than you fear her."*

He had about 100 meters left to run, the distance that determines the world's fastest man. But his whole body felt like it was being turned into a slab of ice: His legs were like concrete, and a blast of cold air produced a burning sensation in his lungs.

Nyx's green, glowing eyes were getting closer.

This time, he said to himself, *I will run THROUGH the finish.*

Tapping into a willpower he never knew he had, Booker reached the gates and fought his way up a circular staircase to the top of the wall.

He raised his torch, igniting a ring of fire that erased the remaining darkness.

"NEXT TIME!" Nyx warned, as she and the last remnants of the storm abruptly vanished.

Some far friendlier faces appeared before him. Ida, Desta, Shen, and Wiri hoisted him up in the air.

Then they all heard the sweetest sound imaginable... the cheering of their fellow young Olympians.

Opa's voice boomed down from the top of Mount Olympus:

"Congratulations... The five of you stepped forward courageously and emerged as leaders among your peers.

"You are a team—a team of five young athletes who have learned to act as one...

"And together you have forged a new Ring Force—one of the many that have fought through the centuries to keep the Olympic flame burning brightly…

"Like the five Olympic rings, you symbolize the union of the major continents… Europe, Asia, Africa, Australia, and the Americas…

"With this honor comes a vital duty... Nyx has been thwarted... But she is not finished... The flame will burn brightly only as long as you keep the spirit of hope alive... as long as you believe in each other... as long as you believe in the best dream of all...

"Endless possibility..."

LET THE DREAMING BEGIN...

"Meow... Meow... MEOW..."

Max's pleas summoned Booker awake. He was suddenly staring at his bedroom ceiling.

Why did his legs feel like he had just run up and down the biggest staircase ever created?

"Yeah, yeah, Max, okay..."

As Booker sat up, he looked over at his poster of Muhammad Ali, and stared at the words across the top:

WHEN YOU BELIEVE IN YOUR DREAM...
ALL IS POSSIBLE.

He began to remember being surrounded by hundreds of kids from all over the world.

Deep inside, he felt different, in a good way. He had the sense he had done something important. Something wonderful.

Then he heard the jangle of keys.

"Hello... Booker?"

Mom.

Oh boy.

Hungry cat, sleeping kid, not good.

"Well, it seems I have a son who ignores rather simple instructions from his mother."

"It's not like that."

"No?... Well, let me see... Cat meowing relentlessly. Boy lazing about in bed... Logical deduction: milk and cat food not purchased... math homework yet to be started... Any explanation?"

"Actually..."

"Yes... I'd like to hear this."

As much as he wanted to tell his mother the truth—how he had triumphed over the goddess of darkness, and her snow leopard, and her many powers, and kept the Olympic flame alive—he very quickly realized that there was absolutely no way she would believe him... and, for that matter, he was thinking maybe all of it never really happened.

"I'm sorry, Mom."

"Okay. How about the track coach?"

Booker's silence provided the answer to that question.

"You know, if your dad were here, he'd want you to join that team. But do whatever you want. I give up."

Then Booker looked down and saw that he was wearing a wristband. At the center was a metal oval, inscribed with a flame.

He suddenly remembered losing the race he should have won, and Sostratas consoling him with a hug.

Maybe coaches weren't so bad.

Coach Popov was loud, but Booker knew he really wasn't mean, and he knew the kids who said

he was really didn't know him at all.

"Don't."

"Don't what?"

"Please don't give up on me... I'm going to join the team... really... You're right, it's what Dad would want me to do."

"You know what, Booker, I don't know why, but I believe you... In the meantime, here's the deal: I'll get the milk and cat food if you start your math homework."

"I'm good with that."

"Really. All of a sudden you like math?"

"Yup... As Mr. Tweedy says, our lives are made of measurements, and you need to understand math so everything will add up."

"Speaking of measurements," his mother said, leaving his bedroom, "how about the eight inches of snow that fell in, like, 30 minutes? Mother Nature is really becoming hard to predict."

His mother picked up the TV remote.

"I have to check the weather before I go out... if we're going to have another freakish storm, I want to make sure I have a hat and gloves."

On the news, giraffes were struggling to walk in accumulating snow.

"That's right, New York," said the weather forecaster, "if you thought today's sudden storm was bizarre, well, take a look at what's happening in Kenya. It's *snowing* at the equator."

Booker's wristband was suddenly getting warmer, and the metal oval with the flame was changing color from silver to gold.

The phone rang in the kitchen.
"Booker, it's for you!"
"Who is it?"
"Someone named Ida... Says it's urgent."

Booker smiled...

He wasn't confused anymore.

He'd been given a very special mission.

The Ring Force was about to be reunited.

A HISTORY OF THE OLYMPICS

The Ancient Olympics began in 776 BC and spanned more than a millennium.

They were held every four years and always at the same site: the valley of Olympia on the southwestern coast of the Greek peninsula.

Tradition holds that everything stopped for the Olympics—even wars. Every four years, a month-long truce was observed while the Games took place.

The Ancient Olympics were abolished in 393 AD. Fifteen centuries later, the Olympics were resurrected by Baron Pierre de Coubertin, a highly educated French aristocrat who believed in the power of sports to promote good health, build character, create joy, and foster international goodwill.

The first modern Olympics were held in Athens, Greece, in 1896. There were 241 athletes from 14 nations.

The first Winter Olympics took place in Chamonix, France, in 1924.

At the 2008 Beijing Summer Olympics, the Games of the 29th Olympiad, there were 10,942 athletes from 204 countries.

London, site of the 2012 Summer Games, is the first city selected to host the Olympics three times.

ABOUT THE AUTHOR

BRIAN BROWN is the Story Editor and Senior Producer of NBC Olympics. The 2012 London Olympic Games will be his twelfth Olympics. He has been lucky to be sent on many wonderful Olympic adventures, including a 36,000-mile South Pacific excursion with stops in 29 places, including the smallest member of the International Olympic Committee: the island of Nauru. Brian also may be the only man to ever visit Sofia, Solnechnodolsk, and Sicily in the same year.

He has been awarded the Olympic Golden Rings three times for excellence in Olympic broadcasting. He's also won a total of 12 Emmys, including an Emmy for Outstanding Documentary, *The Wonders of Rome*; and he's twice won the Dick Schaap Outstanding Writing Emmy award.

Brian is a former reporter for *The New York Times* and *San Diego Union,* and was the supervising producer for HBO's much-acclaimed talk show *On the Record with Bob Costas.* He is also the author of *TV: a novel.* Brian lives in Westchester, New York, with his wife and two children.

Nathan
Love
INDIE 500

ABOUT NATHAN LOVE

NATHAN LOVE is an innovative illustration, design, animation, and concept-development studio that combines the talents of an eclectic group of artists, animators, and producers. Instead of coming together on Mount Olympus, they join forces at their misfit hideout in SoHo, NYC, to concoct their works of imagination and wonder.

Founded in 2007 and driven by a passion to tell great stories and connect with audiences around the globe, Nathan Love develops memorable characters, vividly detailed worlds, and engaging narratives for books, film, television, Web, and video games. Past clients and collaborators include Nickelodeon, McGraw-Hill, Electronic Arts, NBC, and Pop Secret.

To learn more, visit nathanlove.com.

AUTHOR'S ACKNOWLEDGMENTS

Many stories begin, *Once upon a time...*

This story begins and ends with *If...*

If not for the kind patience, indulgence, editorial expertise, and steady support of my NBC Olympic colleagues: Executive Editor **Joe Gesue**, Creative Director **Mark Levy**, SVP Strategic Partnerships **Brett Goodman**, and Olympic President **Gary Zenkel**, this concept would be curling up in the darkness of a file cabinet...

If not for the inexhaustible geniuses at **Nathan Love**... If not for their spectacular art, AND the birthing of a gorgeously illustrated and wondrous new world of characters and setting, AND the tenacious insistence on sharpening the story, this book would not have left the rocket pad...

If you ever have impossible deadlines but yet need a team to do something magical in the world of content creation, write down the names of these guys, including: the firm's indomitable leader and spirited storyteller, Creative Director **Joe Burrascano**... fellow RING FORCE concept developer and master of character and color, Art Director **Anca Risca**... relentlessly marvelous work by lead illustrator **Sigmund Lambrento**, who captured the heart and soul of our characters and their world... Plus voice of reason, in terms of production timeline and narrative tapestry, **Derrick Huang**... With added vital contributions by editor **Matt Cochran** and Executive Producer **James Braddock**.

If not for the nascent NBC News eBook imprint... if not for their instant enthusiasm, warm embrace, defiant defense of my liberal use of punctuation, and my constant flights of fancy... if not for their visual panache, formidable writing and editing skills, and deep knowledge of the publishing business... you would not be holding RING FORCE in your hands...

My undying appreciation to NBC News SVP **Cheryl Gould** and to NBC Publishing VP **Michael Fabiano**, who had the good sense to limit the focus group review of this project to one: his 11-year-old daughter, **Katie**.

I am also indebted to the very perceptive endorsement of **Zeki Hirsch**, the 10-year-old son of NBC News Senior Producer **Inci Ulgur**. As for Zeki's mom, she provided regular therapeutic doses of encouragement and superb polishing while I fueled myself on scrumptious English chocolate during late-night writing episodes while on a long Olympic assignment in South Africa. If not for Inci, the fittingly flowery tribute to the Brooklyn Bridge would have been a casualty many drafts ago.

If not for **Brian Perrin**, the Director of Development for NBC Publishing, this product might still be just a dream and not what it miraculously became because of his Olympic-level willpower: a reality. He is the kind of asset that the smartest companies call a keeper: a deft thinker, writer, artist, negotiator, and cyber-whiz.

Children's book editor and author **Margery Cuyler** added her kind can-do spirit and delicious details... like proposing the evil Nyx should be accompanied by a puma. And though the puma became a snow leopard, Nyx would have been sans un big cat if not for Margery...

If not for the leap of faith made by Rodale books, it's unlikely we would have reached the finish line of our own Olympic literary marathon... Very sincere thanks and gratitude to: **Stephen Perrine**, **Beth Lamb**, **Natalie Lescroart**, **Chris Krogermeier**, **Sean Sabo**, **George Karabotsos**, **Yelena Gitlin Nesbit**, and **Aly Mostel**...

And during this process, I would have been lost without the support and smarts of **Marisa** and **Luke Brown**... If not for my Ring Force stars, my world would not be as it is... filled with abiding joy.